THE PRINCESS
and the
PEANUT ALLERGY

Wendy McClure

illustrated by
Tammie Lyon

Albert Whitman & Company
Chicago, Illinois

Library of Congress Cataloging-in-Publication Data is on file with the publisher.

Text copyright © 2009 by Wendy McClure
Illustrations copyright © 2009 by Tammie Lyon
Hardcover edition first published in the United States of America in 2009 by Albert Whitman & Company
Paperback edition first published in the United States of America in 2019 by Albert Whitman & Company
ISBN 978-0-8075-6619-0 (paperback)
ISBN 978-0-8075-9312-7 (ebook)

Printed in China
10 9 8 7 6 5 4 3 2 1 WKT 24 23 22 21 20 19

Design by Aphee Messer and Mary Freelove

For more information about Albert Whitman & Company,
visit our web site at www.albertwhitman.com.

100 Years of Albert Whitman & Company
Celebrate with us in 2019!

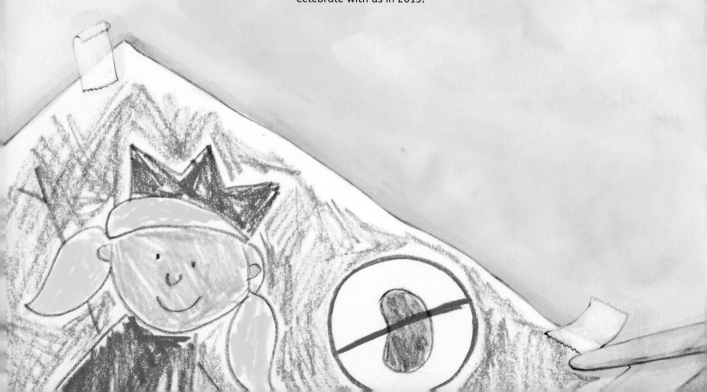

To Chris, with love.
And to Bill Haverchuck too.
—WM

For Nan, thanks for always
admiring the art
—TL

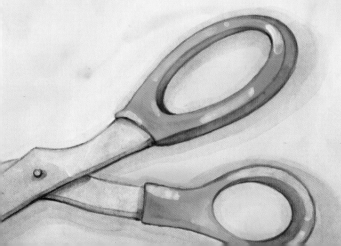

Regina was having her birthday party on Friday.

All the girls in her class were invited. Especially Paula, her very best friend.

Regina had already picked out the perfect cake.

On Monday Regina said at school,
"My party's going to be a princess party."
Both Regina and Paula loved playing
princesses. So Paula could hardly wait.

On Tuesday Regina said, "At my princess party, we're going to play Space Dragons."

And Paula loved playing Space Dragons too, so Paula couldn't wait.

On Wednesday Regina said, "At my princess party, we're going to have a fabulous castle cake made with great big brownie bricks and ice cream cone and candy towers."

And Paula loved cake too.

But then she said, "WAIT!"

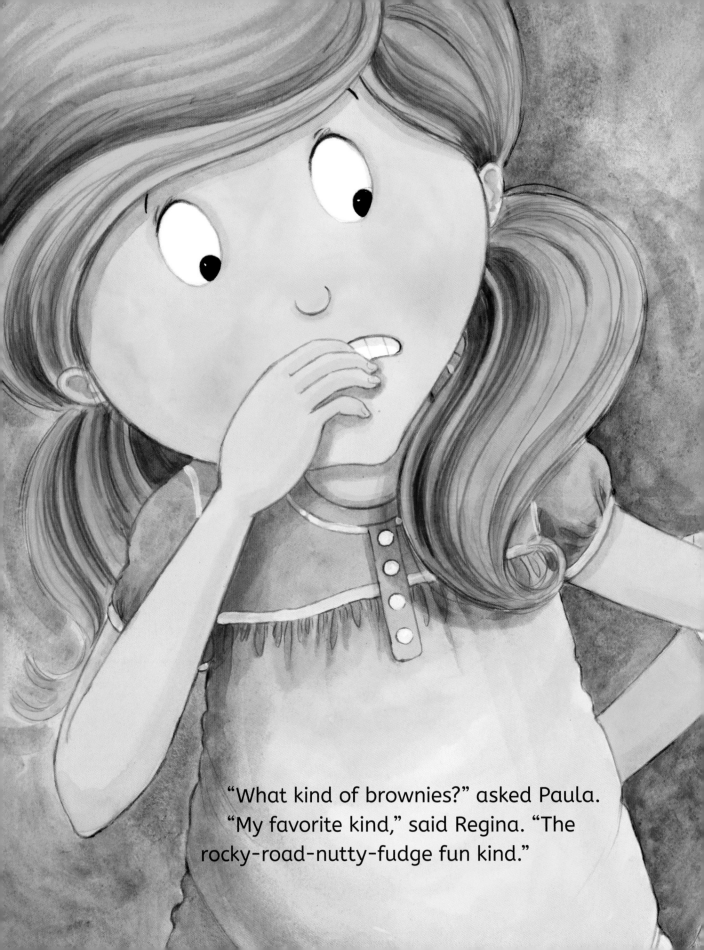

"What kind of brownies?" asked Paula. "My favorite kind," said Regina. "The rocky-road-nutty-fudge fun kind."

Paula panicked. "And what kind of candy?"
"Peanut Butter Bunny Boogaloos," said Regina.

"Oh no!" said Paula. "I can't eat your castle cake.
I'm allergic to the bricks! And the towers will make me sick!
I have a peanut allergy. I CAN'T EAT PEANUTS!"

"Not even peanut butter?" asked Regina.

"Nope," said Paula.

"Not even a peanut?" Regina asked.

"Not a single one," Paula said sadly. "Not even a teeny,
tiny, small one. Once I ate one by mistake, and I had to go to
the hospital! Now I always keep special medicine with me."

"But it's going to be the best cake ever," said Regina. "Can't you pick out the peanuts?"

"No!" said Paula. "I can't eat any foods with peanuts in them. Or *on* them. Or *around* them. It's a really big deal!"

But Regina wanted her CAKE to be the big deal. She said, "You're being a PAIN, Paula! It's *my* party! *I'm* the princess here!"

"Oh yeah?" Paula said.
"Well, maybe I'M the princess too."
"Well, maybe you can't come to my party!"
Regina shouted.
"Well, MAYBE I DON'T WANT TO COME!" Paula yelled.

Regina went home *angry.*

Paula went home *hurt.* (And angry too.)

"I wish I didn't have to tell people about my peanut problem," Paula told her dad.

"*Always* tell people," said her dad. "Don't be a quiet little mouse."

"I wasn't trying to ruin Regina's party," said Paula.

Her dad hugged her. "I know," he said.

"I wish Paula didn't have her peanut problem," Regina told her mom. "But I want my castle cake too!"

She didn't know what to do.

Her mom hugged her. "Let's talk about it tomorrow," she said.

At bedtime, Regina's mom took out "The Princess and the Pea."

"Remember this story?" she asked. "It's one of your favorites."

Regina did remember, and she read it again. As she fell asleep, she thought about how that one LITTLE pea could be such a BIG deal, and how the princess couldn't help feeling it through ALL those mattresses.

Is that how it is to be allergic? Regina wondered the next morning. Even the littlest, teeny, tiny bit of something could hurt?

She wouldn't let that little something hurt her friend.
And she wouldn't let it ruin the party either!

On Thursday after school, Regina and her mom went to the bakery.

Regina told the woman exactly what she wanted for her perfect cake.

"Can you do it, please?" she asked. "It's a really big deal!" And Regina told her why.

"Don't worry, we can do it," the woman said. "We've made special cakes like this before."

When they got home, there was one more thing for Regina to do. She called Paula.

"At my princess party, we're going to have a fabulous castle cake made with great big brownie bricks," she said. "And there won't be any peanuts ANYWHERE in the cake."

"There won't?" asked Paula.

"There won't," said Regina.

"Thank you," said Paula. "You're the best princess ever."

"So are you," said Regina.

And it was the best
princess cake ever.

A Note to Parents and Friends of Children with Food Allergies

Food is part of our culture, our socialization, and our recreation. But it is estimated that one in twenty children has a food allergy. For these children, simple pleasures such as participating in holiday meals, going Halloween trick-or-treating, going to a restaurant, or even attending a best friend's birthday party pose health and social challenges.

Although a child can become allergic to virtually any food, the most common offenders are peanut, egg, milk, tree nuts (walnut, cashew, etc.), wheat, soy, fish, shellfish, and sesame. A food allergy occurs when the immune system, the part of the body designed to fight infection, mistakenly "attacks" food proteins, leading to a number of illnesses including sudden allergic reactions. For reasons we do not fully understand, we are seeing an increase in food allergies. Peanut allergy is especially problematic as it is often severe and rarely outgrown.

The child with a food allergy who consumes sometimes even a tiny amount of the wrong food can experience allergic symptoms including an itchy mouth, hives, itchy and swollen skin, nausea, and vomiting. Severe symptoms can include throat tightening, wheezing, trouble breathing, poor blood circulation, and unconsciousness. A severe allergic reaction, anaphylaxis, can, unfortunately, be fatal.

People with food allergies need to do two things: avoid the foods to which they are allergic and be ready to treat a severe allergic reaction with an injection of epinephrine, a medication that reduces the severe symptoms, allowing time to get to an emergency room. Adults must keep a child with food allergies safe by carefully reading product ingredient labels, asking questions in restaurants, knowing about how food can become tainted by allergens through cross-contact during meal preparation (e.g., using a knife in peanut butter and then in jelly), and ensuring children do not share unsafe foods.

A child with a food allergy can do most everything that other children can do, except eat the food to which he or she is allergic. With education, understanding, preparation, and a sense of community, children with food allergies can live safely and happily.

Scott H. Sicherer, MD
Jaffe Food Allergy Institute
Mount Sinai School of Medicine, New York City
Author, *Understanding and Managing Your Child's Food Allergies*